This book belongs to:

_____

The Yum Yums

By: Tiffany Lyn

In a very magical place, in a far and distant land, lives a group of tiny people known as the Yum Yums.

The Yum Yums love to sing and to dance, to laugh, and to play. But most of all, the Yum Yums love to eat!

They eat **Yum Yum** custard for breakfast, followed by mid morning brunch. There is even **Yum Yum** custard served for lunch.

But every day at six, when the tall clock tower rings, the entire kingdom comes to have a magical feast of yum with their king.

As little boys and girls on earth finish their dinner plates, the skies of Yum open wide and rain down all the children just ate. Fruits and veggies, meat, and grain were amongst the yummy treats that the sky would rain.

Over time, however, boys and girls began to eat less. Meaning there wasn't enough food raining down for the king to host a Yum Yum fest.

So the great hall was locked. The clock tower no longer rang. And the Yum Yums had to eat Yum Yum custard when dinner time came.

The king became very sad, so sad that he got sick. And the great Dr. Uhm told the kingdom that something had to be done quick!

All the Yum Yums gathered but no one could figure out what to do. Without the feast of Yum, the king would never stop being blue.

But little tiny Yim had an idea to bring back the king's joy. "What if I asked every child to finish their dinner, starting with a little girl, followed by a little boy?"

The Yum Yums agreed. Possibly
this could work. So they sent little
Yim to Jordan's house first.

Jordan Taylor, who was about the age of three, refused to eat her dinner even though her mother tried continuously. "Come on Jordan, just taste it. I promise it's yummy."

Her mother tried the airplane, followed by
the choo-choo train; yet nothing seemed to work.
So little Yim appeared to Jordan and said in a small, tiny voice,
"Here, I'll eat one first." He took a big bite. "Uhmm, that's
yummy! Will you try some with me?" And with that Jordan
took a bite, then two, then three.

It wasn't before long, that her entire plate was empty.

Little Yim danced with joy, making Jordan happy too. And from that day forward Jordan ate all her dinner everyday because that's what little Yim was counting on her to do.

From house to house little Yim went, helping the children to eat their fruits, veggies, dairy, grain, and meat.

Finally when little Yim returned home, much to his surprise, the great hall was unlocked and everyone was inside.

The king was well again. He was
excited and filled with joy, that
all the children were eating again,
every girl and every boy.

The kingdom gave a big Yum Yum cheer
for Yim as there was much to celebrate.
All the fruits, veggies, meat, and grain
now graced their dinner plates.

www.ingramcontent.com/pod-product-compliance
Lightning Source LLC
Chambersburg PA
CBHW041009170626
46815CB00002B/231